For Michael— **C. F.**

To the Bianchi family, with love!— **J. A.**

SIMON & SCHUSTER BOOKS FOR YOUNG READERS
An imprint of Simon & Schuster Children's Publishing Division
1230 Avenue of the Americas, New York, New York 10020
Text copyright © 2017 by Claire Freedman
Illustrations copyright © 2017 by Giuditta Gaviraghi
Originally published in Great Britain in 2017 by Simon & Schuster UK Ltd
Published by arrangement with Simon & Schuster UK Ltd
First US Edition 2017
All rights reserved, including the right of reproduction in whole or in part in any form.
SIMON & SCHUSTER BOOKS FOR YOUNG READERS is a trademark of Simon & Schuster, Inc.
For information about special discounts for bulk purchases, please contact
Simon & Schuster Special Sales at 1-866-506-1949 or business@simonandschuster.com.
The Simon & Schuster Speakers Bureau can bring authors to your live event. For more information or to book an event,
contact the Simon & Schuster Speakers Bureau at 1-866-248-3049 or visit our website at www.simonspeakers.com.
Book design by Tom Daly
The text for this book was set in Artcraft URW.
Manufactured in China
0517 SUK
2 4 6 8 10 9 7 5 3 1
CIP data for this book is available from the Library of Congress.
ISBN 978-1-4814-9904-0
ISBN 978-1-4814-9905-7 (eBook)

I Love You, Baby!

Claire Freedman
Illustrated by Judi Abbot

A Paula Wiseman Book
Simon & Schuster Books for Young Readers
New York London Toronto Sydney New Delhi

Three tiny words—
I love you—
seem too small for me to show
how much I love you, Baby,
but I just want you to know. . . .

I love your sleepy wake-up smile,
as we start our day.

I love our morning cuddles,
and the way we laugh and play.

I love your funny one-tooth smile,
your kissable sweet nose,

that tickly-wickly tummy,
and those perfect wriggly toes!

I love the wonder in your eyes
at all the things you see.

The scent of pretty flowers
as you hold one up to me!

I love you, love you, love you,
so much more than you can guess.
And nothing you could ever do
would make me love you less.

When days are gray and chilly,
you're my sunshine, little one.

We'll curl up with a storybook,
for warm and cozy fun!

Hide-and-seek and peekaboo—
we find fun in all our play.

If there are tiny tumbles,
my love kisses them away!

I love you when you run and jump,
and make a lot of noise.

I love you when you're quiet
and calm, or play games
with your toys.

I love to keep you safe and dry
in thunderstorms and rain.

I love our puddle splashing
when the sun bursts out again!

My bright bundle of happiness,
you mean the world to me.

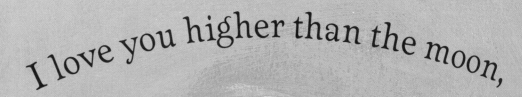

I love you higher than the moon,

and deeper than the sea.

Each day is an adventure.
You'll make friends and have such fun.

But I'm always close beside you,
if you need me, little one.

So snuggle down and close your eyes,
the night is soft and still,

I love you, love you, love you,
and I always, always will!